E

FOURTEEN DAYS

A fine of TWO CENTS will be ch
for each day the book is kept ov

3-19	8-22	
10-29	6-20	
11-9	7-7	
12-8	6	
4-11	3-	
5-3	6-	
7-2	10-	
4-18	3.25.	
7-29	7-	
11-11		
8-7		
12-8		
-23		

Grayfur

Published by Raintree Steck-Vaughn Publishers, an imprint of Steck-Vaughn Company

Library of Congress Cataloging-in-Publication Data

Potter, Tessa.
Grayfur, the story of a rabbit in summer / story by Tessa Potter; illustrations by Ken Lilly.
p. cm. — (Animals through the year)
Summary: Startled by a noise while grazing peacefully in the summer sun,
Grayfur must overcome her fear and protect her young kitten against a fierce predator.
ISBN 0-8172-4621-5
[1. Rabbits — Fiction.] I. Lilly, Kenneth, ill. II. Title. III. Series.
PZ10.3.P4835Gr 1997
[E] — dc21 96-38989
CIP AC

With thanks to Bernard Thornton Artists

The author would like to thank Dr. Gerald Legg of the
Booth Museum of Natural History, Brighton, for his help and advice.

Color separated in Switzerland by Photolitho AG, Offsetreproduktionen, Gossau, Zurich.

Printed and bound in the United States

1 2 3 4 5 6 7 8 9 0 IP 00 99 98 97 96

Grayfur

The Story of a Rabbit in Summer

Story by Tessa Potter
Illustrations by Ken Lilly

RAINTREE
STECK-VAUGHN
PUBLISHERS
The Steck-Vaughn Company

Austin, Texas

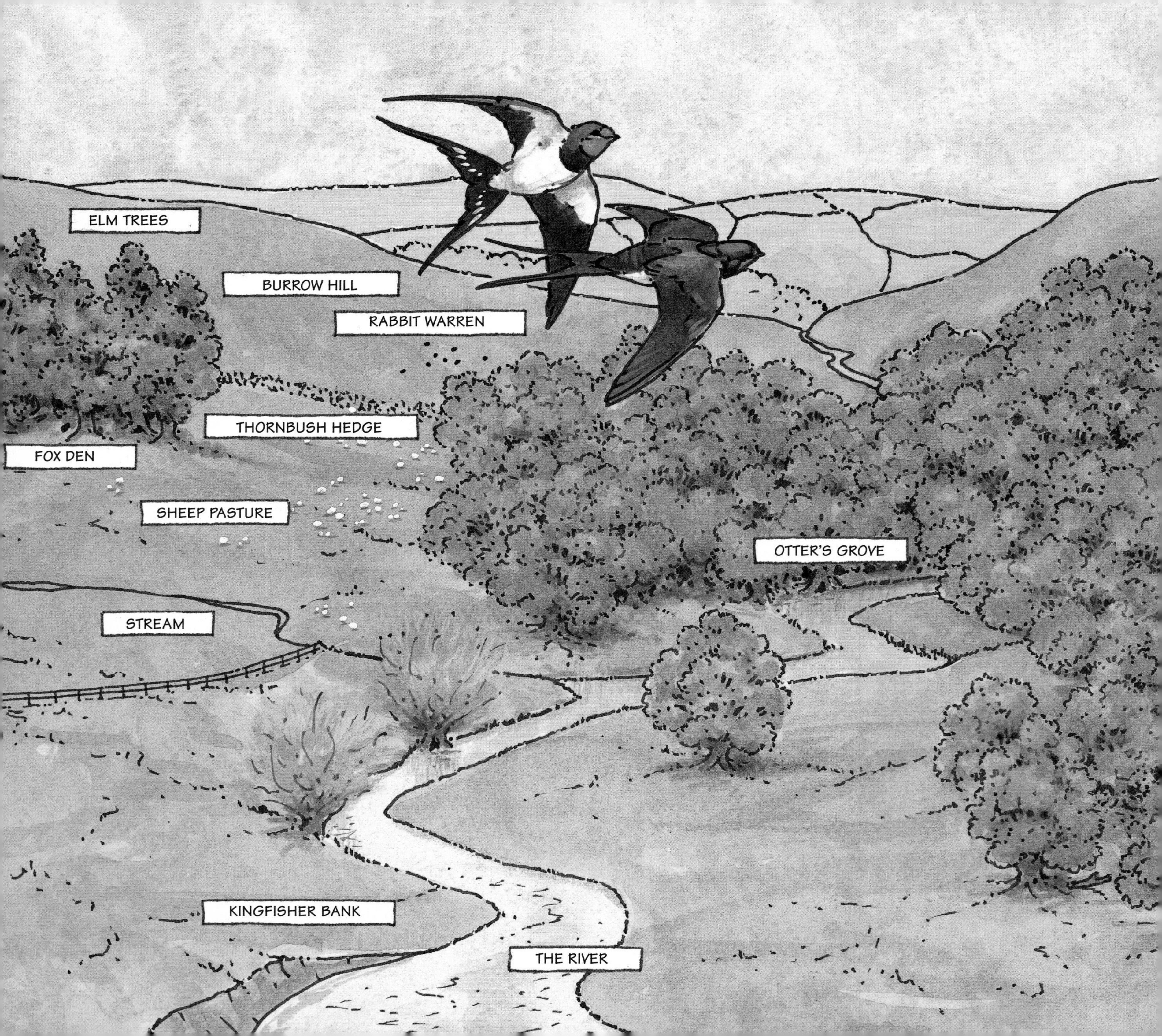
ELM TREES
BURROW HILL
RABBIT WARREN
THORNBUSH HEDGE
FOX DEN
SHEEP PASTURE
OTTER'S GROVE
STREAM
KINGFISHER BANK
THE RIVER

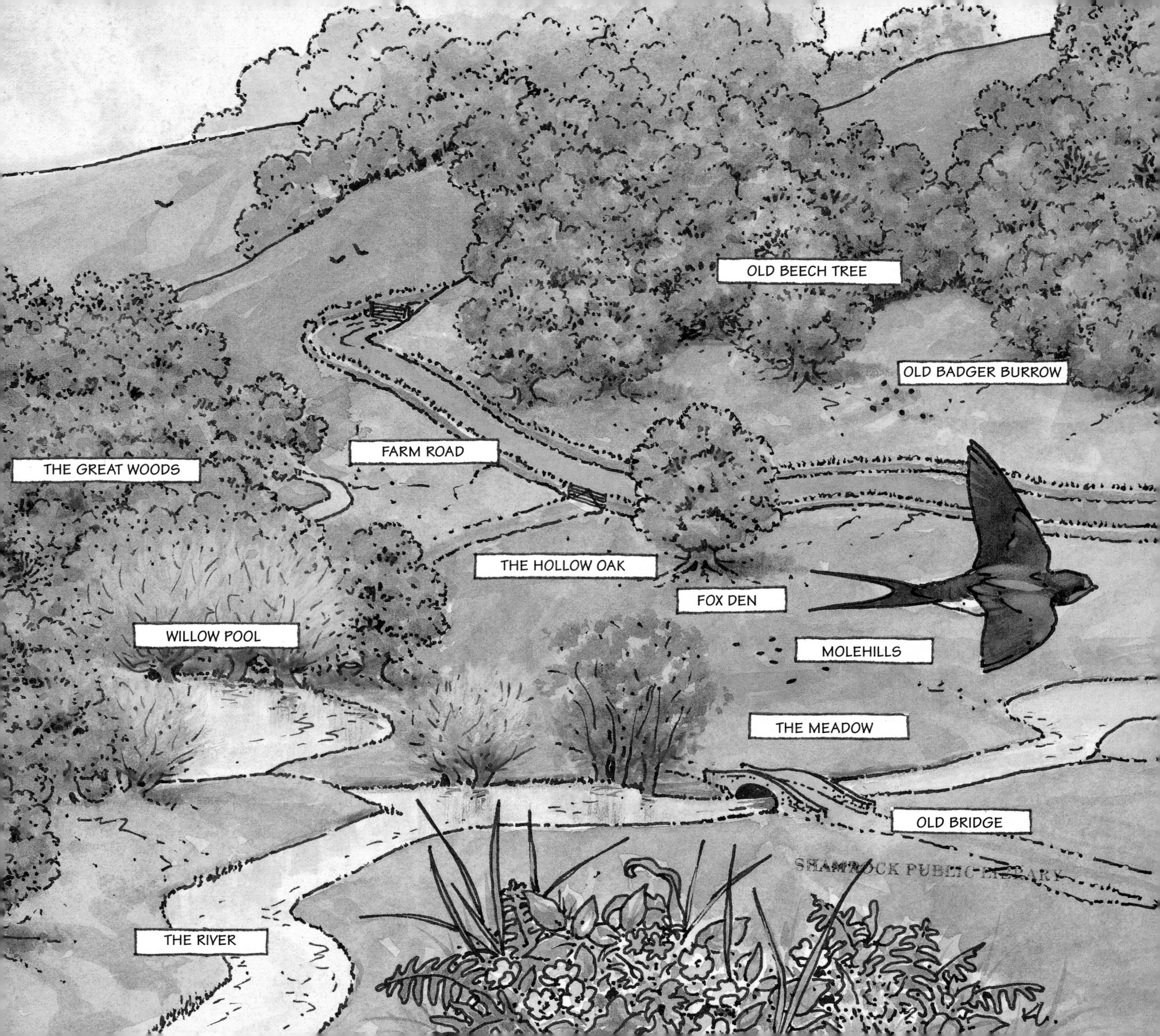
OLD BEECH TREE
OLD BADGER BURROW
FARM ROAD
THE GREAT WOODS
THE HOLLOW OAK
FOX DEN
WILLOW POOL
MOLEHILLS
THE MEADOW
OLD BRIDGE
THE RIVER

It was warm, sweet summer in the Great Woods. A young weasel had just finished a meal of wood mouse and curled up to sleep.

Out on Burrow Hill, Grayfur dived into her burrow for the third time that night. The thumping paws of other rabbits warned her of otters slipping through the long grass.

Grayfur lay still and listened, protecting her three kittens. There was a snuffling, scratching sound near the entrance to her burrow, but then the noise passed. The otters were returning to the river. They'd been catching eels in the old dike and had no thoughts of rabbit that night. From above Sheep Pasture came the angry snarling and barking of two young male foxes. At last, the night grew quiet. Grayfur fell asleep.

She awoke in the early morning. She was hungry. She crept to the edge of the burrow and looked out. She heard birds above and a bee buzzing — quiet, familiar sounds. It was safe to come out.

Grayfur led her kittens through the hedge and down the grassy bank. A small mole who had blundered onto the path in front of them turned and scurried back to the woods.

Everything was peaceful. Grayfur began to eat. Two of the small rabbits played by the hedge, but the smallest one began to wash himself under the oak tree.

"Chouk! Chouk!" The noise of the thrush calling its mate startled them. Grayfur quickly thumped with her back legs in warning. The two young rabbits nearest the hedge scampered up the bank, but the smallest rabbit lost his balance and toppled over.

In that instant, Grayfur saw him — it was the young weasel, and he was deadly.

The little rabbit crouched low, too frightened to move. Grayfur's heart pounded — she wanted to run. But she had to protect her young. She would fight to save them. The weasel was uncertain what to do. He'd hoped to grab a small rabbit without being seen. He crept forward.

Grayfur ran at the weasel.
With all her strength she
struck him with her back legs.
There was a flurry of fur.

The weasel hissed and swiveled around, trying to grab Grayfur. But she bit him hard with her sharp front teeth, kicking wildly at him.

Spitting with pain and rage, the young weasel backed away and turned and ran into the Great Woods.

Grayfur crept back to the burrow with her kitten.

She lay in the warm, dark nest and waited for the pounding in her chest to grow quiet. In a while she would take her kittens out again to feed, but for now they would stay in the safety of the burrow.

Look back at the story. Can you find...

A **click beetle** escaping from a shrew. When threatened, it lies on its back and then springs high in the air away from danger.

A **buttercup**.

A **small tortoiseshell butterfly** laying her eggs under a stinging nettle leaf.

A **titmouse** carrying some caterpillars in its beak.

A **field mouse** in its nest of bark and grasses.

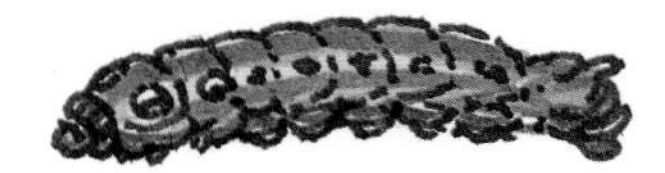

An **elephant hawkmoth caterpillar** trying to frighten away a young blackbird. It swells up its head to show off its eyespots.

A **long-eared bat** out hunting insects.

A **field poppy**.

A **garden spider** in her web. The male spider taps a special signal to tell her he is not an insect. Otherwise she may eat him.

A speckled **moth** hiding against the bark of a tree.

A **mole** escaping into its tunnel.

A **nut weevil**. It lays its eggs inside a new hazel nut. When the tiny grub hatches, it feeds on the nut.

A **moth caterpillar**. This caterpillar protects itself by rolling up in a leaf.

A **swallow**.

A **harebell**.

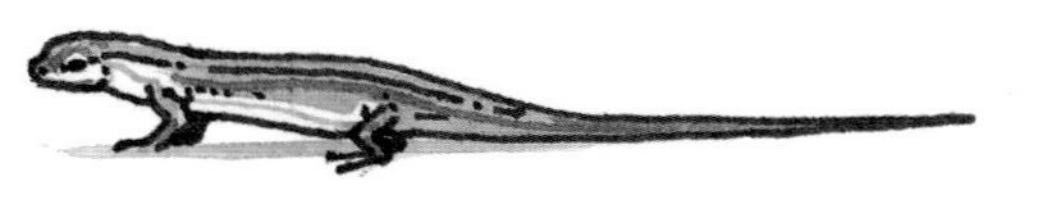

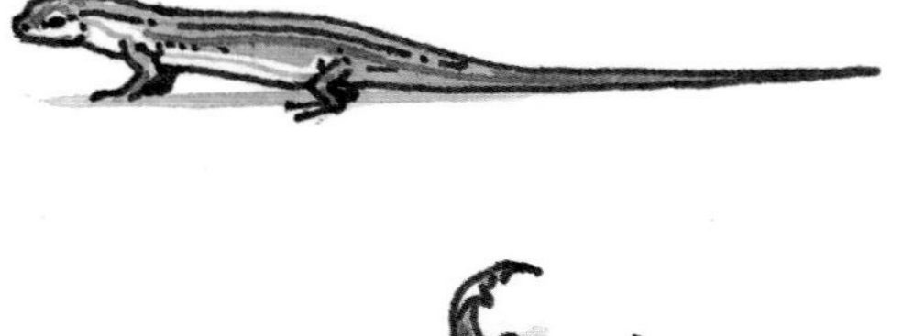

A **common wall lizard** and a **stag beetle** hanging on the thorns of a thornbush. They have been caught by a shrike and stored in its larder.

Honeysuckle.

A **crab spider** hiding on a flower. When an insect comes to get nectar, the spider grabs it with its front legs and bites it with its fangs.

A **dog rose**.

A **female nursery web spider**. She has laid her eggs and spun a silken tent over the cocoon. She will stand guard until the tiny spiders hatch.

A **white admiral butterfly** collecting pollen and nectar.

A **sparrow hawk** on its plucking block. It uses an old tree stump to tear up and eat small birds.

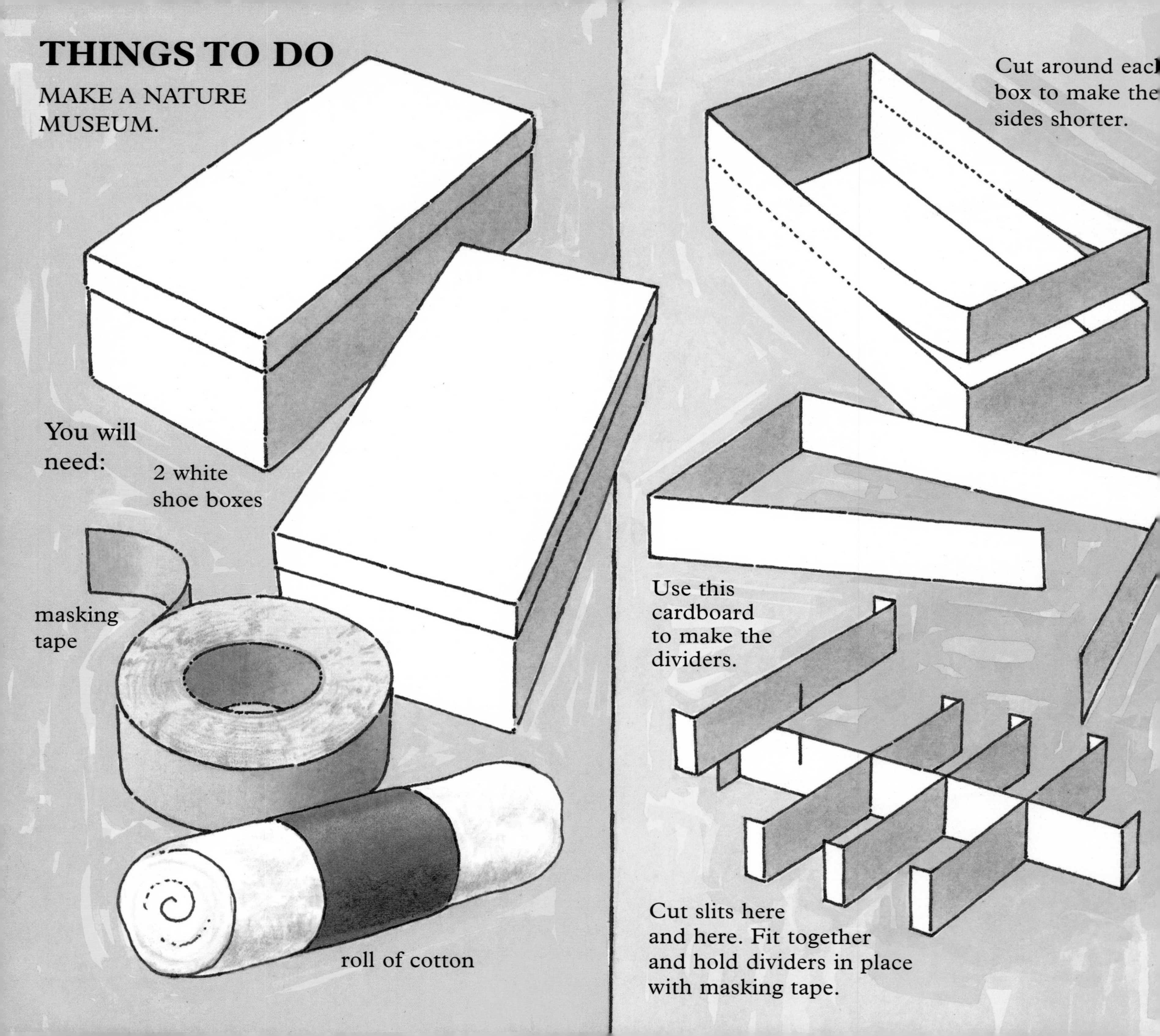
THINGS TO DO
MAKE A NATURE MUSEUM.
You will need:
2 white shoe boxes
masking tape
roll of cotton
Cut around eac
box to make the
sides shorter.
Use this cardboard to make the dividers.
Cut slits here and here. Fit together and hold dividers in place with masking tape.

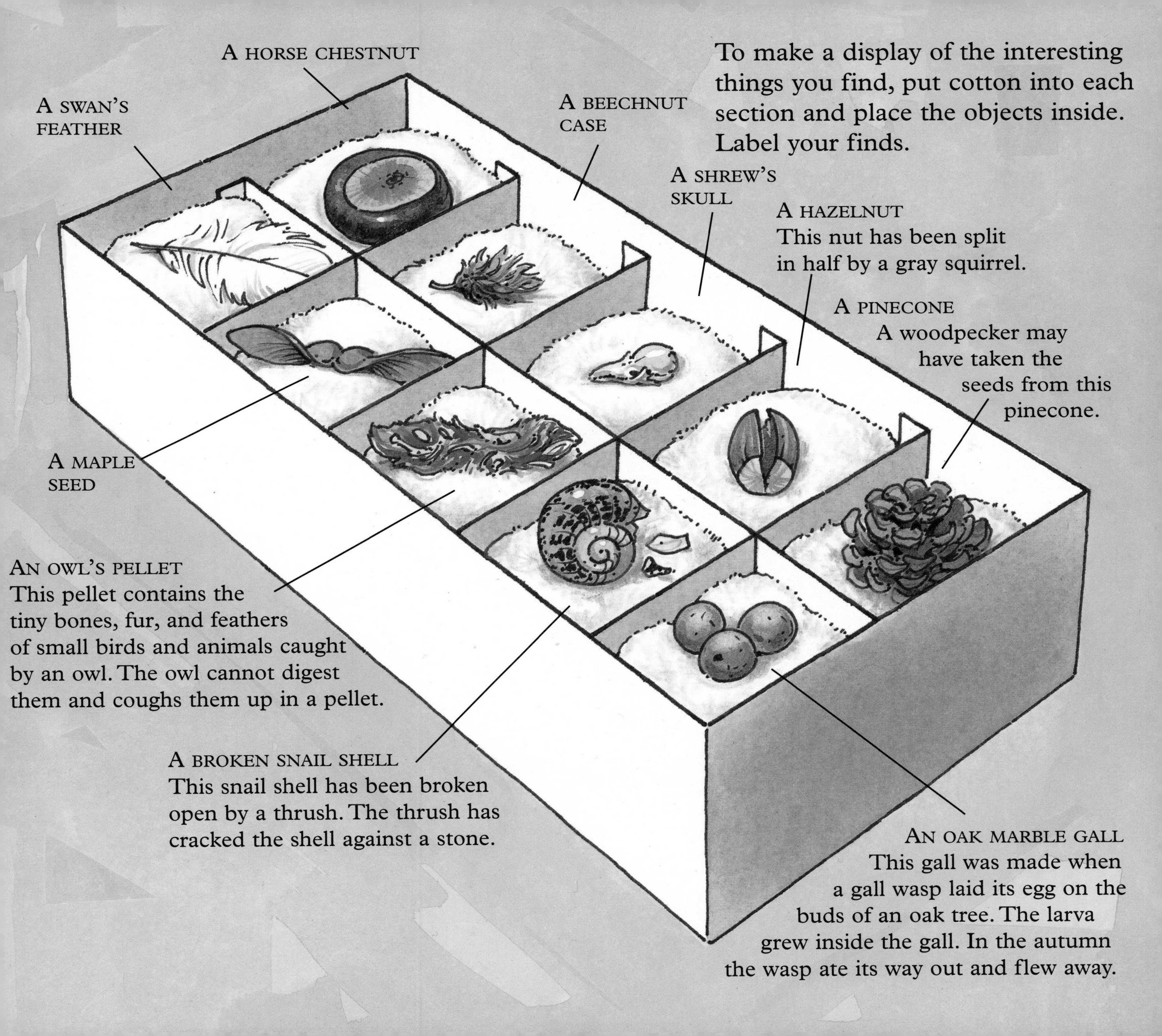
To make a display of the interesting things you find, put cotton into each section and place the objects inside. Label your finds.
A HORSE CHESTNUT
A SWAN'S FEATHER
A BEECHNUT CASE
A SHREW'S SKULL
A HAZELNUT
This nut has been split in half by a gray squirrel.
A PINECONE
A woodpecker may have taken the seeds from this pinecone.
A MAPLE SEED
AN OWL'S PELLET
This pellet contains the tiny bones, fur, and feathers of small birds and animals caught by an owl. The owl cannot digest them and coughs them up in a pellet.
A BROKEN SNAIL SHELL
This snail shell has been broken open by a thrush. The thrush has cracked the shell against a stone.
AN OAK MARBLE GALL
This gall was made when a gall wasp laid its egg on the buds of an oak tree. The larva grew inside the gall. In the autumn the wasp ate its way out and flew away.

MORE ABOUT RABBITS

Books

Barkhausen, Annette and Geiser, Franz. *Rabbits and Hares*. Gareth Stevens, 1994

Bryant, Donna. *My Rabbit Roberta*. Barron, 1991

Coldrey, Jennifer. *The World of Rabbits*. Gareth Stevens, 1986

Hall, K. *Bunny, Bunny*. Childrens, 1990

Hearne, R. *Rabbits*. Rourke, 1989

Lepthien, Emilie U. *Rabbits and Hares*. Childrens, 1994

Mayo, Gretchen W. *Here Comes Tricky Rabbit*. Walker and Co., 1994

Watts, Barrie. *Rabbit*. Dutton, 1992

Williams, Margery. *The Velveteen Rabbit: Or, How Toys Become Real*. Holt, 1983

Videos

Exploring the World of Mammals. (30 min.) Busch Entertainment, Batavia, Ohio: Video Treasures, 1992

Life on Earth. Episode 10. (58 min.) BBC/Warner Brothers. Films, Inc. distributor. Naturalist David Attenborough on mammals, 1988

See How They Grow. (30 min.) Includes wild animals, rabbits, foxes. Dorling Kindersley. Sony Kids' Video, 1995

First published in 1996 by Andersen Press